by **Summer Waters**

Silver Dolphins

DOUBLE DANGER

HarperCollins *Children's Books*

Prologue

A short way from the cliffs a dolphin swam frantically through the water, her voice calling out in shrill whistles and clicks. Hearing her distress, Spirit, the leader of the dolphin pod, quickly swam to her side.

"Wait," he clicked, swinging his magnificent silver body round to stop her from swimming away. "What's wrong?"

"It's Sunny," sobbed the dolphin. "I only stopped for a minute, but when I turned back Sunny had vanished."

"He can't have gone far," Spirit soothed her. "Stay calm. We'll soon find him."

Spirit drifted in the water for a moment, his

senses tuned to the sea. Then smiling, he said, "Follow me."

He led the dolphin away from the cliffs, then dived down to the seabed. Suddenly, a group of dolphins sped past, herding a shoal of fish. With their prey corralled into a tight ball, the dolphins pounced, catching the fish in their mouths.

"Sunny," clicked Spirit, when the fish had all gone. "Your mother was worried about you."

The little dolphin squeaked with surprise.

"Spirit," he clicked, bowing his head. Then, eyes shining with excitement, he added, "Did you see that? Did you see me catch my first fish?"

"I did," clicked Spirit kindly. "But next time

you go off with your friends, remember to tell your mum."

Sunny blushed, but his mother wasn't cross, just dazed.

"I didn't know he was ready to fish," she stammered.

"Our children are full of surprises," said Spirit. "They learn quickly."

Spirit shivered as a strange feeling swept over him. He sensed surprises and difficult choices ahead for the Silver Dolphins. But they were fast learners too. Spirit was confident they would make their decisions wisely.

Chapter One

Sophie was waiting for Antonia at the end of her drive. Antonia grinned and her feet gave a little skip as she hurried towards her friend. Sophie had been on holiday and now she was back for the final two days of the summer term.

"Hi," she called.

"Hi," said Antonia, running the last few steps and giving Sophie a hug. Linking arms, she asked, "How was Jersey?"

"Brilliant," Sophie sighed. "I wanted to stay longer, but Mum said everyone had to go back to work, including me."

"I should think so too," Antonia teased.

Sophie had only been away for a week, but Antonia thought it felt like much longer. She'd missed having her around.

"I bet we won't be doing anything interesting. It'll be boring stuff, like tidying and emptying our trays ready to move up to Mrs Howard's class in September."

"Well, I'm glad you came back. It wasn't the same without you," said Antonia.

"I missed you too. I wish you could have

come to Jersey with us. You'd have loved it.
The beaches were fantastic. And guess what?
I even had a go at surfing! I wasn't any good,
though."

Sophie chattered on, hardly pausing for
breath. Antonia didn't mind. She was glad to have
Sophie back. They'd been best friends forever.

"We went to a pottery and I bought you
something." At last Sophie paused as she
started to shrug her school bag off her
shoulders. "You can have it now."

Just then a familiar sensation swept over
Antonia, making her body tingle with
anticipation. Spirit, her dolphin friend, was
about to call. Antonia's heart quickened. This
was tricky. She wanted to stay and chat, but
she had to answer Spirit's call immediately.

Then she remembered that they were on their way to school. Antonia did some quick thinking.

"Er, thanks, but I've just remembered, I left my packed lunch at home. I'm sorry, Sophie, but I'll have to go back and get it." Antonia felt her face redden at the fib.

"I'll come with you," said Sophie. "You can take your present home. I wasn't happy about bringing it to school anyway, in case it got broken."

The silver dolphin charm Antonia always wore round her neck started vibrating. She covered it with her hand, even though she knew that Sophie wouldn't notice. Only a Silver Dolphin could hear the dolphins' call. Silver Dolphins were guardians of the sea. They had special magical abilities to help them care for the oceans and the creatures living there.

Antonia stopped walking. Her heart was racing, but she forced herself to stay calm. "That would be fun, but there's no point in us both being late. You go on ahead and tell Miss Brown and my mum where I am. They'll worry if I don't turn up on time."

Sophie sighed. "It must be a pain having a mum who works in the school office. Trust you to forget your lunchbox today! I've got so much to tell you."

"I'm sorry, Soph. I'll be as quick as I can."

Antonia felt guilty at letting Sophie down, but at the same time wished she would hurry up and go to school. Spirit needed her. The dolphin charm thrumming against her neck suddenly gave a shrill whistle.

Spirit, I hear your call. I'm on my way.

Antonia thought the words, not daring to say them aloud.

"See you in a bit, then," said Sophie sadly.

Antonia waved and the girls walked in opposite directions. When Sophie was out of sight, Antonia turned down the alley that led to the coastal path. School bag bumping against her back, she jogged all the way to Gull Bay. The beach was deserted. Slipping out of her sandals and socks, and leaving them hidden behind a rock with her bag, Antonia ran across the soft white sand to the sea. The water was cold and she winced as she splashed further out. When the water reached her waist she took a deep breath, then swam. At once her legs melded together, kicking like a dolphin's tail. Using her hands as flippers, Antonia powered along, her streamlined body arching as she leapt and dived in and out of the sea, just like a real dolphin. The silver dolphin charm was still whistling, but now she could hear something else. A soft whisper, that was gone before Antonia could make out what it was.

"Spirit?" she clicked.

"Silver Dolphin," he replied.

"I'm on my way."

"Be quick, Silver Dolphin."

Antonia swam faster out of Gull Bay, across Sandy Bay and round the headland. She kept going until she reached a tiny cove that she remembered visiting once with Spirit's son, Bubbles. Spirit was waiting for her near the cliffs, a short distance from the cove's entrance. He bowed his magnificent silver head. Cai, Antonia's Silver Dolphin friend, trod water close by and shot Antonia a triumphant grin. Antonia hesitated. She wasn't nearly as in awe of Spirit as she used to be, but sometimes she still felt shy in his presence. Spirit came forward and rubbed her nose in greeting, and immediately Antonia relaxed.

"Thank you for coming, Silver Dolphins," said Spirit. "Follow me and I'll show you why I called."

Spirit dived under the water.

"I got here first," said Cai cheekily, as he

and Antonia dived after the dolphin.

"Well done," clicked Antonia good-naturedly. She didn't remind Cai that she'd had further to swim. Antonia was a very powerful Silver Dolphin; there were lots of things that she could do that Cai never would.

They swam down through the blue-green water until they reached a bed of eelgrass, its long green stems swaying gently with the swell of the ocean.

"Oh!" Antonia gasped.

A supermarket trolley lay on its side, crushing a large area of the eelgrass.

"How did that get here?"

"Someone probably pushed it off the cliff," said Cai.

"It's causing a lot of damage," clicked

17

Spirit. "Come closer and you'll see what I mean."

Antonia and Cai skimmed slowly over the trolley, noticing the snapped and damaged eelgrass poking through its metal bars. Movement caught Antonia's eye. She stared at the trolley, then pointed excitedly.

"A seahorse!"

Antonia stayed very still as she watched the tiny yellow seahorse. Its elegant neck and bowed head looked so like a real horse in miniature, that she half expected the creature to have legs and hooves instead of a long curled tail, anchoring it to a blade of eelgrass.

"There's more," said Cai suddenly. "Look, they're dancing."

Two seahorses were swimming in an

elaborate circle, their spiny bodies dipping and swaying in the water.

"Aunty Claudia says seahorses are becoming rarer," said Cai, who was living with his aunt while his parents worked in Australia. Claudia ran a marine conservation charity called Sea Watch and until recently, she had been a Silver Dolphin too.

"That's why I called you," said Spirit gravely. "This is a new breeding ground for the seahorses, but they won't survive without the eelgrass."

Antonia's grey-green eyes flashed angrily.

"That one's dead already," she said, pointing to a seahorse just visible under the trolley's bright red handle. The seahorse's eyes were dull and half of its tail was missing.

"It looks like it was crushed."

She grasped hold of the trolley and began to lift it.

"Help me," she panted.

"Wait!" said Cai. "You'll cause more damage if you're not careful. Let's think about how we're going to do this."

Antonia let go of the trolley.

"Sorry," she said ruefully. "I got carried away. If I take this end and you take the other, we can lift it straight up without causing any more damage."

"But what will we do with it then?" asked Cai. "The beach in that cove nearby is surrounded by cliffs. There's no path."

Antonia pushed her long blonde hair away from her face.

"I know," she said. "We'll swim it to Claudia's beach. Thank goodness it's private. Mum will ground me forever if I'm seen out when I should be at school."

Chapter Two

Raising the abandoned trolley from the eelgrass beds was more difficult than it looked. Even though it was small, it was heavy and awkward to manoeuvre in the water. The eelgrass snagged in the trolley's metal sides and snaked round its wheels, holding it back.

"Careful," said Antonia, concerned for the

two dancing seahorses, which suddenly changed colour, then dashed away as the trolley shifted position.

Cai held it steady while Antonia swam round, freeing as much of the eelgrass as she could. With Spirit's help, they slowly swam the trolley to the surface.

"We could do with some help," said Cai. "It's going to be tricky swimming with this."

The water began to vibrate, then like a mini tornado, a column of water spun from the surface, as Bubbles leapt out of the sea. He was followed more sedately by his sister, Dream, and their mother, Star.

"Bubbles," clicked Antonia happily. She was so pleased to see him again, she wanted to turn a somersault. But that would mean letting go of the trolley, so she splashed the water with her tail-like legs instead.

"Hi Dream, hello Star; it's good to see you too."

"Hi," said Dream, swimming up and gently rubbing noses with Antonia, then Cai. Turning to Star, she asked, "Can we help the Silver Dolphins, Mum?"

"Hello," clicked Star, greeting Antonia and Cai with a friendly nose rub.

"Can we help?" asked Bubbles impatiently.

Star hesitated. "I don't think it would be a good idea," she clicked. "That thing is hard and scratchy. It could easily damage your soft skin. Let the Silver Dolphins deal with it. Their hands are more useful than fins on this occasion."

"Aw, Mum!" clicked Bubbles. "Please let us help. We'll be really careful."

But Star wouldn't allow it. "It's too dangerous. You can play with the Silver Dolphins when they've finished their task," she said firmly.

Bubbles cheered up immediately. "Sprat or seaweed tag?" he clicked.

"Neither," panted Antonia. "Sorry Bubbles, but we've got to go to school when we're done. We're late as it is."

"What's school?" asked Bubbles.

"It's a place where children go to learn things," Antonia explained.

Bubbles looked puzzled. "Can't your parents teach you what you need to know?" he asked.

"Our parents are too busy working," said

Cai. "I don't even live with mine right now. They're in Australia."

Bubbles stared at Cai with his mouth open. "Humans," he clicked, slowly shaking his head. "You make things so complicated."

Antonia and Cai laughed loudly.

"Too right," said Cai.

Spirit helped the Silver Dolphins swim the shopping trolley towards Claudia's beach. Bubbles swam alongside, occasionally turning somersaults or suddenly diving underneath the trolley.

"Bubbles!" said Star in a warning tone. "I'll take you out to sea if you don't behave."

Bubbles rolled his eyes when his mother wasn't looking and Antonia stifled a giggle. Star was as strict as her own mother, but she loved them both dearly. Thinking about Mum made Antonia uneasy. How long had they been gone? It was difficult to gauge time when she was a Silver Dolphin. And, although it seemed to go more slowly, Antonia was worried that she might be so late for school she'd need a better excuse than forgetting her lunchbox.

At last, Claudia's beach came into view. There was lots of nose-rubbing and ruffling hair with flippers as the dolphins said goodbye. Bubbles high-fived Antonia and Cai with his tail.

The Silver Dolphins dragged the trolley ashore. It was even more awkward to move on land than it had been in the sea. The sand jammed the trolley's wheels until eventually they gave up trying to push it and carried it over to the Sea Watch boat. Antonia pulled a hair-tie out of the pocket in her dress and swept her damp hair into a ponytail. It was the only thing to show she'd been swimming in the sea. The Silver Dolphin magic had left her clothes as dry as if she'd been sunbathing.

"Hopefully no one will notice my wet hair," she said.

"I'm sure they won't," agreed Cai, pulling on his shoes. "Where did you leave your shoes? We'll ask Aunty Claudia to take us there in the car before she drops us at school."

Antonia brightened. "Thanks," she said. "It'll be quicker than walking."

Chapter Three

Claudia drove Antonia to Gull Bay and then on to school. She left Cai at home, promising to take him in later.

"It'll look suspicious if you both arrive late together," she said, her sea-green eyes twinkling.

School had not long started, but Antonia

had missed the register and Miss Brown sent her to the office to see Mrs Lee, who was in charge of signing in latecomers. Antonia smiled cheerfully at her mother, but Mrs Lee gave her a stern telling-off.

"Don't ever do that again," she ranted. "You are supposed to walk straight to school. If I can't trust you to go where we've agreed, then you won't be allowed out alone."

"I only went home to get my lunchbox. I asked Sophie to tell you where I was going," Antonia protested.

"That's not the point!" said Mrs Lee. "You've been gone ages. What took you so long?"

"I got a stitch from running," mumbled Antonia. She hated telling lies, but being a

Silver Dolphin meant making difficult choices.

"I'm grounding you this afternoon," said Mum, when she eventually ran out of things to say. "Meet me here after school. I'll walk you home with Jessica."

"Mum!" exclaimed Antonia. "You can't ground me. I promised I'd go to Sea Watch. We're getting the guillemots ready for their release back into the wild."

The guillemots had been at Sea Watch for several weeks, since a minor oil spill in Sandy Bay damaged their feathers.

"Sea Watch will survive without you for one afternoon," said Mum firmly. "Now go back to class. You've wasted enough lesson time already."

Cai was disappointed that Antonia wasn't

allowed to go to Sea Watch, but Sophie was pleased.

"Can I come home with you?" she asked. "We haven't been round to each other's houses after school for ages."

Antonia's face reddened. "I'd love you to. I don't want you to think that you can only come round when I'm not allowed to go to Sea Watch, though."

"Don't be silly," said Sophie. "We're better friends than that!"

Jessica, Antonia's little sister, was ecstatic to have both Antonia and Sophie walking home with her.

"Can I play with you?" she asked. "I'm seven now. It was my birthday when you were away, Sophie."

"I know," said Sophie. "I can't believe you'll soon be in Year Three."

"So can I play with you?"

"For a little bit," said Sophie kindly.

At home, Antonia took Sophie straight up to her bedroom. Sophie's gift from the Jersey pottery was a beautiful dolphin figurine with a blue and gold glaze. Antonia put it in pride of place on her dressing table. They talked for ages, mostly about Sophie's holiday in Jersey. Sophie also had her sketch book with her and showed Antonia some of the sketches she'd done for her latest art project: painting pictures of the cats that roamed around Sandy Bay. Then Jessica came barging in, demanding that the girls played with her too. She wanted to play hide-and-seek, so everyone went

outside to hide in the garden. Sophie played
four games before deciding she'd better go
home. Antonia went to the side gate with her
to wave goodbye and Jessica trailed after
them. When Sophie had gone, she followed
Antonia indoors and upstairs to her bedroom.

"You like dolphins, don't you?" she asked,
noticing the present from Sophie on the
dressing table.

"They're my favourite animal," Antonia
agreed as she pulled her swimming bag out of
the cupboard. It was squad night. Luckily
Mum hadn't grounded her for that too!
Antonia packed her bag with the things she
needed.

"Is it because you swim like a dolphin?"

Antonia's heart missed a beat as she spun

round to face her sister. What did Jessica mean?

"Naomi's sister is in your class at school. She calls you the dolphin girl because you're brilliant at swimming."

"Oh!" Antonia smiled. For a wild moment, she thought Jessica had discovered the secret of the Silver Dolphins.

"Can I try your necklace on?" asked Jessica, reaching out to touch it.

Antonia drew back. "No, Jess, you know my necklace is special."

"Please," begged Jessica, making her green eyes go wide. "I want to see if the magic works for me too."

There was a funny rushing sound in Antonia's head. She tried to speak, but her mouth was so dry that her voice came out in a croak.

"What do you mean?"

"I know your dolphin charm is magic. Ages ago, you said it made you swim better," said Jessica innocently.

Antonia met Jessica's eyes, choosing her words carefully as she spoke. "My charm isn't magic. It's lucky. It gives me confidence, so I swim better when I'm wearing it."

"Can I touch it then," said Jessica, "for luck?"

"No." Antonia quickly hid the dolphin charm inside the collar of her school dress.

"You're mean!" Jessica's eyes welled up with tears.

Antonia was suddenly ashamed of herself.

"Don't cry," she said, hugging Jessica's stiff little body. "I'm not being mean. This is my lucky charm. The luck only works for me. You'll have to find your own thing. Why do you need luck anyway?"

Jessica sniffed. "I want to be brilliant at swimming, just like you. And I want to learn to surf too."

"Then you need to practise," said Antonia. "Practising is much more important than luck. Look, I'll tell you what. Once school's broken up we'll ask Mum to take us to the swimming pool and I'll help you practise."

"Will you?" Jessica wiped a hand across her eyes. "Thanks, Antonia. You're the best sister in the world."

Jessica skipped off. Antonia stared out of

her attic window, hardly registering the wonderful view of Sandy Bay. A small seed of worry nagged at her like an aching tooth.

By tea time, Antonia could hardly eat the spaghetti bolognaise Mum had cooked. Twirling a strand of pasta round her fork, she let it drop back on to the plate. Had she totally convinced Jessica that her charm wasn't magic? To most people the dolphin charm looked like an ordinary necklace. Only a Silver Dolphin knew it was more than that. But what if Jessica was a Silver Dolphin? Antonia hoped not. Her sister was far too little. Sometimes the work was dangerous and often it required making difficult decisions. How would Jessica answer the dolphins' call, when she wasn't allowed to go anywhere on her own?

There was another reason why Antonia didn't want Jessica to be a Silver Dolphin too. Being a Silver Dolphin made Antonia feel special. She didn't want to share the secret with her little sister. Poor Jess; she'd called Antonia the best sister in the world, but Antonia knew she wasn't. She was selfish and mean. She pushed her half-eaten tea away from her.

"Are you feeling all right?" asked Mum.

"I've got a headache," said Antonia truthfully, because her head was spinning.

"Better go and sit quietly for a bit," said Mum.

"Thanks." Gratefully, Antonia fled up to her room.

She sat on her bed, gently stroking her

silver dolphin charm. She loved the way it felt like a real dolphin.

After a while, her head cleared and she felt calmer. Talk about overreacting. Of course Jess wasn't a Silver Dolphin. What a mad idea! With a lighter heart, Antonia ran downstairs to see if Mum had saved her any pudding.

Chapter Four

Walking to school with Sophie the next morning, Antonia's feet felt like they were floating on air. Finally, it was the last day of term. Straight after lunch – an end-of-term picnic on the school field – the holidays started. Six whole weeks of freedom! Antonia couldn't wait.

Miss Brown's desk was a mountain of gifts and Antonia added her own to the pile – a pretty notebook made from recycled paper and a pen with a clay starfish on the end. The morning was a blur of last-minute tidying, followed by a final assembly. Lunch was a noisy, cheerful affair. The Year Sixes, who were leaving for secondary school, came round collecting signatures on their school sweatshirts and cardigans. Antonia drew a dolphin on her friend Emily's and the big girl squeaked in delight.

"Are you going to Sea Watch after school? Wait for me then," she said.

Emily talked non-stop on the way to Sea Watch. She'd brought her camera with her to take some photos of the guillemots before they were released.

"Aunty Claudia thinks we can let them go next week," said Cai. "They should be properly acclimatised by then."

"A clima-whattie?" asked Emily.

"Acclimatised; it means getting them used to being outside again."

Claudia was pleased to see everyone. As they tidied their school bags into a cupboard, she drew Antonia to one side.

"Bad luck about yesterday. I hope you weren't in too much trouble?"

"I was a bit," Antonia admitted. "I'm just glad school's finished. Now I can stop worrying about what to do if Spirit calls in the middle of a lesson."

"That would be awkward," agreed Claudia. "But you'd find a way round it."

"How? What if it happens next term?"

Claudia smiled and immediately Antonia knew what her answer would be. Staring into Claudia's sea-green eyes she thought, *I have to work it out for myself.*

Without speaking, Claudia answered, *You are the Silver Dolphin.*

Antonia wondered if she should mention her suspicion about Jessica, but decided against it. Of course Jessica wasn't a Silver Dolphin. It was just a silly thought.

Claudia put Antonia and Cai to work, moving the guillemots from their indoor pens to an outdoor aviary. To transport the birds, she gave them a special cardboard box with handles and air holes, and a thick pair of gloves each.

"If the birds are frightened, they might try and bite you, so remember to talk to them in a low calm voice and don't make any sudden movements," said Claudia.

Antonia was very fond of the guillemots. There were nine survivors, each with their own cheeky personality. Antonia's favourite was a bright-eyed bird who always had a lot to say.

"You sound just like my neighbour's cat," Antonia told her, as she gently transferred the bird to the cardboard box. "Stop complaining until you see where I'm taking you. I think you're going to like it."

The guillemots did like being outside. They

hopped around, exploring their new surroundings, before settling down to preen themselves.

"Let's go and tidy up the indoor pens, so they're ready for the birds when they come back inside this evening," suggested Cai.

Antonia agreed, but as they headed back to the Sea Watch building, she knew they weren't going to be able to do the job right then. A tingling sensation was sweeping through her and Antonia sensed that Spirit was about to call. Cai was reaching for the door handle when the silver dolphin badge pinned to his school polo shirt began to vibrate. Surprised, he stood for a second, before flashing a look at Antonia.

"Ready?" he asked.

Antonia nodded and side by side they ran for Claudia's private beach. Antonia's own charm was also vibrating, its silver tail thrumming against her neck.

Not life-threatening, she decided as the charm beat in a steady rhythm.

They ditched their shoes in the Sea Watch boat and ran into the sea. Antonia's charm broke into a high-pitched whistle and she whistled back. "Spirit, I hear your call."

Cai whistled too, but stopped as the water reached his waist. Thrusting himself forward, he began to swim. Antonia swam alongside him, enjoying the moment her legs melded together and began kicking like a tail. She could never tire of becoming a Silver Dolphin. Joyfully she leapt in and out of the sea,

arching her body as she skimmed the water. After a bit, Antonia realised she'd drawn ahead of Cai and her old dilemma of whether to wait for him or not played in her mind.

"You go on," Cai panted.

Antonia shook her head. "It's not urgent. Anyway, I've got a feeling I'm going to need your help."

Cai slid an admiring look her way.

"Wish I could do that," he said. "I can't tell how urgent a call is."

Antonia blushed, cross with herself for voicing her thoughts. She loved being such a powerful Silver Dolphin, but she didn't want Cai to think she was boastful. They swam in silence until, rounding the headland, Cai said, "I can feel vibrations. Do you think it's Spirit?"

Antonia nodded. She'd felt the vibrations too. They seemed to be coming from the same direction as the cove where Spirit had shown them the seahorse colony. She hoped the seahorses were all right. Anxiously, Antonia swam faster. Cai increased his pace too and they reached Spirit together. He was waiting in the same place as the day before. As soon as they'd rubbed noses in greeting, Antonia asked, "Is it the seahorses?"

"Yes," clicked Spirit. "There's more rubbish in the eelgrass." He dived underwater, and Antonia and Cai followed him.

On the edge of the eelgrass beds lay an abandoned plastic bin. "Oh, no!" Antonia exclaimed. "Look at the damage it's done!"

Chapter Five

The bin was the sort the coastguards put on the beach during the summer months, with a moulded top and holes in the side to post litter through. Antonia and Cai slowly swam round it, assessing how best to remove it from the eelgrass without causing further damage. A seahorse drifted past and Antonia stopped to stare as, with a curl of its tail, it gracefully anchored itself to a stalk of eelgrass.

"Did you know it's the boys that have babies?" said Cai. "The female lays over a hundred eggs in a pouch on the male's tail, but hardly any of the baby seahorses survive after they hatch."

"I'm not surprised when people do idiotic things like this," said Antonia. "I'd love to know how the bin got here. It had to be deliberate."

Cai nodded his dark curly head. "Let's find out who's doing this. We've got heaps of time now we're on holiday."

The bin was empty and easy to move, and the damage it had caused wasn't as bad as they'd first thought. It had completely flattened a patch of eelgrass, but luckily the roots were still intact. Antonia and Cai swam with the bin to the surface.

"Are we taking it back to Aunty Claudia's beach?" Cai asked.

Antonia nodded.

"Would you like Bubbles and Dream to help you?" asked Spirit. "The bin doesn't seem to have any sharp bits."

Antonia and Cai grinned. "Yes, please," they said.

Spirit opened his mouth and called for his children in a series of short clicks. A few minutes later, Antonia spotted two dolphins swimming towards them, their bodies flashing in silver arcs.

"That was quick!" she exclaimed, when Bubbles and Dream reached them. Bubbles clicked a laugh. "We've been here all along, hiding. Dad told us not to get in the way."

They all rubbed noses in greeting.

"Seaweed tag, when the Silver Dolphins are finished?" asked Bubbles hopefully.

Spirit shook his head. "Not today. I'm taking the whole pod fishing, out at sea."

Bubbles was disappointed. But once Spirit had left, he invented a game of swimming under the bin while it was being pushed. That proved easy so Bubbles livened things up by walking on the water on his tail, alongside the bin. Soon there was lots of splashing and squealing, as whoever's turn it was struggled to stay on the sea's surface. Bubbles took particular delight in suddenly crashing back down into the sea, splashing everyone with salty water.

"No more!" panted Antonia eventually. "I'm completely out of breath."

"Flipper Feet," teased Bubbles. "You need to practise."

That's what I told Jessica, thought Antonia, guiltily touching her dolphin charm. She made a mental note to take her little sister swimming soon. The bin was less awkward to swim with than the supermarket trolley and, with Bubbles and Dream helping, it wasn't long before they reached Claudia's beach. The dolphins said goodbye, Bubbles high-fiving Antonia and Cai with his fin, while Dream rubbed her nose against theirs.

"See you soon, Silver Dolphins," clicked Bubbles, as he and Dream swam back out to sea.

Salty water poured from Antonia and Cai as they emerged from the sea, but soon they were damp again with spray from the bin as they rolled it ashore.

They left the bin by the gate that led from the beach and went to look for Claudia. She was in the garden, talking to a builder who'd come round to quote on building a deep-water pool, to rehabilitate creatures like the guillemots and injured seals. When the builder had gone, Claudia helped them put the bin by the garage, ready to take back to the beach.

The rest of the afternoon was spent doing

routine jobs. At the end of the day, Antonia, Cai and Emily brought the guillemots back inside for the night. Emily was often one of the last volunteers to leave Sea Watch and Antonia walked some of the way home with her.

"What time are you coming tomorrow?" Emily asked when they parted.

"Early," said Antonia. "I thought I'd get up at the same time as I do for school."

"You're keen!" said Emily. "I'm going to have a lie-in for a change."

Antonia hated staying in bed in the morning. There was more fun to be had than sleeping. She wasn't the only early bird in her family. Jessica was an early riser too and the following morning, she stormed into

Antonia's room demanding to be taken swimming.

"Not today, Jess," said Antonia, jumping out of bed and searching for her clothes.

"But you promised," wailed Jessica.

"I *will* take you, but I didn't promise to take you today. It's the first day of the holidays and I'm going to Sea Watch."

"Pleeeeaase," begged Jessica. "You went to Sea Watch yesterday. Please take me swimming."

Mum came in to see what the noise was about and settle the argument. "I don't have time to take you to the pool today. Why don't you go to Sea Watch with Antonia and I'll take you swimming on Monday?"

"Mum!" exclaimed Antonia. "She can't

come to Sea Watch. She's too young."

"I'm seven now. That's not too young," said Jessica, scratching her head.

Antonia felt a jumble of emotions. She loved her sister dearly, but she could also be a big pain. Antonia didn't feel ready to share Sea Watch with Jessica. Her hand strayed to her dolphin charm. She stroked it gently, comforted by the feel of its life-like body.

"I'm sure Jessica could manage half a day," said Mum firmly. "I'll ring Claudia and ask. No, not now, Jessica. It's far too early. Stop pulling your hair like that and go and brush it. And clean your teeth while you're at it."

Excitedly, Jessica skipped from the room.

"Your little sister isn't so little any more," said Mum, smiling. "Cheer up. There's plenty of room for everyone at Sea Watch."

Antonia smiled bravely. "I don't mind her coming, really."

"Good girl," said Mum. "Breakfast in ten minutes."

Alone in her room, Antonia felt awful. She wished she could honestly say she didn't mind about Jessica going to Sea Watch, but she did. Picking up a hairbrush, Antonia combed her long blonde hair. She brushed hard, refusing to think about another more worrying thought that buzzed in her head like an irritating fly. It was bad enough Jessica helping out at Sea Watch. But what if she became a Silver Dolphin too?

Chapter Six

To Antonia's relief, Claudia didn't make her look after Jessica. Instead she paired her little sister with Emily, getting them to prepare a cage for an injured seagull. Antonia and Cai were asked to research seahorses on the Internet. Claudia was keen to learn more about the new colony they had found.

"Seahorses are quite rare these days. They're shy creatures and not enough is known about their behaviour. By studying them in the wild, we can help to protect them and their environment," Claudia explained.

In no time at all, Antonia and Cai found the website for a charity dedicated to conserving seahorses.

"That one," said Antonia, pointing excitedly to an image onscreen. "That's the same as ours."

"Then they're Spiny Seahorses," said Cai, reading the caption beneath the picture.

Claudia was pleased with the information and said she would ring the seahorse charity when she had a spare moment. "They might want to send a diver to check out the colony

for themselves," she added.

"How will you say we discovered them?" asked Cai.

Claudia grinned. "I shall tell them a local person found the seahorse colony when out diving. It's not that far from the truth."

The volunteers stopped halfway through the morning for a break. Antonia was handing out plastic cups of squash and tea from a tray when she noticed Jessica was missing.

"Where's Jessica?" she asked Emily. She was sharper than she meant to be, annoyed that she was worrying about her little sister.

"Don't panic," said Emily. "She's gone outside to talk to the guillemots. She's so good with them. It's like the birds understand what she's saying."

Antonia went cold and her hands began to tremble. She quickly handed Emily a cup of tea to stop it from spilling.

"Thanks." Emily looked surprised. "I was going to have squash, but tea will make a nice change."

Antonia's mind was a whirl as she finished handing round drinks and biscuits. Jessica liked animals, but Antonia hadn't noticed she was that good with them. The next-door neighbour's cat had actively avoided Jess since, as a toddler, she'd coloured his white patches pink with a lipstick borrowed from Mum's handbag. Wondering what else there was about Jessica she didn't know, Antonia dumped the tray on a table to go outside. Claudia stopped her.

"Is everything all right?"

"Yes, I think so. I was just going to check on Jess."

"Jessica's fine," said Claudia. "I'd leave her be."

"But..." Antonia desperately wanted to confide in Claudia that Jessica might be a Silver Dolphin, only her fears sounded selfish and mean.

Reaching out, Claudia took both of Antonia's hands in her own. Her face was serious as she stared deeply into Antonia's grey-green eyes.

Would it be so very bad?

Antonia felt her face colour. Were her thoughts that easy to read?

Yes, no. I mean... I don't know.

Antonia blushed deeper, knowing that her own attitude hadn't been very nice.

I'm sorry. It'll be fantastic if Jessica is a Silver Dolphin. It's just a surprise. So... is she?

An enigmatic smile played on Claudia's lips. Frustrated, Antonia forced herself to smile back. Claudia was bound to tell her to work it out for herself.

What will be, will be.

"Oh!" Antonia was so surprised, she didn't realise she'd answered Claudia aloud.

What did that mean?

She stared at Claudia, but she only replied by gently squeezing Antonia's hands.

"Go and have a drink and a biscuit before they're all gone," she said kindly.

The morning passed quickly. Antonia was so busy she hardly noticed Jessica and when Mum arrived at lunchtime to take her home, Antonia had to admit that having her little sister at Sea Watch wasn't so bad after all. Surprisingly, that evening when the family were having tea, Jessica was more interested in talking about going swimming on Monday than her time at Sea Watch. She continued to talk about it all weekend, almost driving Antonia mad.

"Come and help me find a lucky charm," Jessica called, early on Monday morning.

Walking into Jessica's room, Antonia's eyes widened at the mess. Jessica had emptied the contents of her cupboard on to the floor and was rummaging through a pile of toys.

"These are no good," she declared, waving at an abandoned pile of cuddly animals. "They're too big and they'd go soggy in the water." She picked up a miniature plastic dog, eyed it speculatively, then tossed it aside. "No, that's not right, either."

"Jess," said Antonia, squatting down beside her. "Jessica, listen to me. You don't need a lucky charm to swim well. You need to practise."

"You've got one," said Jessica, pushing her brown bobbed hair away from her face.

"That's different. My dolphin charm is lucky, but I was a good swimmer before I got it because I practised loads. I still do."

Jessica scratched her head. Screwing her

face into a pout, she said, "I want a lucky charm too."

Antonia sighed. "Well, you haven't got time to find one now. Mum said to get your swimming things ready. We're leaving in ten minutes."

"But I need something to bring me luck." Jessica looked stricken. "Can I touch your dolphin? I'll be really careful. Please, Antonia?"

Antonia stood very still. How could she refuse when it was obviously so important to Jessica? Antonia sort of knew how her sister felt. Touching something for luck was another way of convincing yourself that you had the courage to perform the task ahead of you.

"Go on then."

Jessica's face lit up. "Thank you, Antonia," she whispered.

Slowly she came forward, then stretching out her right hand, touched Antonia's silver dolphin charm.

"Oooh!" Jessica kept her fingers on the charm as her eyes closed in ecstasy. "It feels just like a real dolphin."

Chapter Seven

The swimming trip went very well. For the first time ever, Jessica swam a whole width of the pool without armbands. She was overjoyed and convinced that Antonia's dolphin charm had brought her good luck.

"You did it yourself, Jess," Antonia told her.

"Yes, but your charm helped," said Jessica stubbornly.

Antonia wished she could share her sister's excitement, but her stomach was a bubbling pot of emotion. She could hardly eat the sausage and chips Mum treated them to at one of the beachside cafés. As soon as she was home, she shut herself in her bedroom and stared out of her attic window. Now the summer holidays had officially started, Sandy Bay was busier than ever, with hoards of swimmers near the shoreline and a scattering of motorboats further out. Antonia was so deep in thought, she completely missed the sensation that Spirit was about to call. The first moment she realised that he needed help was when her dolphin charm juddered to life.

The charm vibrated against her neck, then broke into a high-pitched whistle. Antonia jumped guiltily, shocked that she was so wrapped up in her own troubles, she'd tuned out her sixth sense. The charm whistled again and Antonia heard another sound. The soft whispering noise she'd heard before, but like the first time, it disappeared before she could work out what it was.

Spirit, she whistled. *I hear your call.*

She rushed out of her room, almost colliding with Jessica, who was carrying two of her doll's house people.

"Will you play with me?" Jessica offered Antonia a doll.

"Later." Antonia dived round her sister and fled down the stairs.

"What's all the thumping?" Mum came out of the kitchen and frowned at Antonia.

"Sorry, I just remembered something. I need to go to Sea Watch to sort it out."

"What, right now? Can't you just ring them?"

"Er, it's something I need to do," Antonia stammered. Self-consciously, she covered her dolphin charm with a cupped hand. Her mother shouldn't be able to see it moving or hear the ear-splitting whistle, but Antonia wasn't taking any chances.

Mum sighed. "I don't know! You spend more time at Sea Watch than at home these days. Go on then, but don't stay too long. I want you back for tea."

"Thanks, Mum." Antonia gave her a quick

hug, then pulled on her sandals.

"Slow down," said Mum, restraining Antonia with her hand. "If it's that urgent, I can take you there in the car."

Antonia pulled open the front door, looking at Mum over her shoulder.

"Thanks, but I'd rather walk," she said.

Jessica stood halfway down the stairs. Their eyes met. Jessica held the look and Antonia felt a flush of red creeping up her neck.

"Got to go," she said, jumping outside and shutting the door firmly behind her.

Closing her mind to any unwelcome thoughts, Antonia ran all the way to Gull Bay. It was the nearest beach and hopefully quieter than Sandy Bay beach, a well-known tourist spot. The sun shone from a clear blue sky and beads of sweat trickled down her face. Her dolphin charm was beating quickly and Antonia sensed that Spirit's call was urgent. Hoping it wasn't the seahorses again, Antonia jumped down on to the sand. She pulled off her sandals and walked briskly to the furthest edge of the cove. There were no tourists sunbathing here. Antonia left her shoes under an overhang of rock where the cliff met the beach. She looked around, but everyone further up the beach was too busy having fun to notice her. Casually, she sauntered into the sea. The water was cool and refreshing, and she shivered with delight. When it reached her waist, Antonia swam. Almost immediately her legs melded together.

Knowing she mustn't be seen, Antonia had to fight the urge to leap in and out of the water with sheer delight. Instead she dived down and swam underwater to find Spirit.

Antonia sensed she was being called towards the seahorse colony. She continued swimming underwater until she was clear of first Gull Bay, and then Sandy Bay. Her dolphin charm thrummed against her neck and anxiety made her swim faster. What had happened this time? It was a relief finally to spot four heads bobbing in the water. The three black shiny ones Antonia recognised as Spirit, Dream and Bubbles. The fourth head was Cai's. So where was Star? Antonia powered on, and was slightly out of breath as she joined her friends.

There was no friendly greeting from Spirit or banter from Cai about how he'd beaten her again. The situation was obviously too serious. Spirit nudged her hand with his nose and clicked, "Follow me," before diving underwater.

Antonia glanced at Cai and he pulled a face to show he knew as little as her.

"Hurry, Silver Dolphins," urged Bubbles.

They swam after Spirit through the clear water until the eelgrass beds came into sight. Antonia fixed her attention on the waving stems of grass and at once she spotted Star. She was coasting slowly above the eelgrass. Her eyes were anxious and she held her head unnaturally still, as if moving might be dangerous.

"Star!" cried Antonia, hurrying towards her. Sensible Star barely moved. A trickle of blood stained the water around her. Wedged on her nose, like an old-fashioned gas mask, was a broken glass bottle.

Chapter Eight

Antonia stroked the side of Star's face while quickly assessing how bad the accident was. "What happened?" she asked.

"We came to check on the seahorses," said Spirit. "And we discovered more rubbish in the eelgrass beds – mostly cans and bottles. I was going to call for you when Star noticed

one of the seahorses giving birth right in the middle of it all. She was worried the babies might drift inside the bottles and cans and get stuck, so we decided to clear the immediate area. Most of the things were easy to move, but we didn't notice the broken bottle. Star was pushing a can caught up in the eelgrass when she slipped and ended up getting her nose stuck in it.

"The cut isn't that deep," said Antonia eventually. "The big problem is how to remove the bottle without making it worse."

"Butter," said Cai automatically.

"Pardon?" asked Antonia.

"Butter," repeated Cai. "That's what my West Indian grandma would suggest."

"Butter, of course!" exclaimed Antonia.

"Mum used it on Jess once when she got her arm stuck in between the bars on the garden gate. It made her arm slippery enough to pull free. But we haven't got any butter."

"There's seaweed, though," said Cai thoughtfully. "Seaweed's slippery. You stay with Star, while I go and find some."

"We'll come too," clicked Bubbles and Dream.

Spirit stayed with Star, swimming in an anxious circle around her. Antonia clicked soothing noises while stroking Star's face. Gradually, the panic left Star's eyes and she relaxed. In no time at all, the water began to vibrate. Cai, Bubbles and Dream returned, the dolphins triumphantly towing strips of seaweed from their fins and Cai carrying a square polystyrene container.

"You'll never guess what we found," said Cai, swimming to Antonia's side.

"Butter?" she asked hopefully.

"Nope. Tomato ketchup." Cai flipped open the lid of the container to reveal the congealed remains of a beefburger, liberally coated in ketchup. "We found this floating in the sea. There were several containers. It looks like there's been some kind of party. Ketchup's slippery. I thought it might work better than the seaweed."

"It's worth a go," said Antonia. She smeared the ketchup on her fingers, disdainfully wrinkling her nose as she rubbed it on to Star's face. It was a tricky job to get the ketchup under the broken glass without cutting herself.

Star never flinched. In a dignified silence, she held herself still as Antonia worked the ketchup around her silvery nose. When there was no more left in the carton, Antonia surveyed her handiwork.

"I think that should do it," she clicked. "Are you ready, Star?"

Star gave a slight nod of her head.

"Do you want help?" asked Cai, tucking the polystyrene container under his arm.

"Yes, please," said Antonia.

Together they eased the bottle from Star's nose. It stuck at first, but by gently twisting it this way then that, the bottle gradually slid free. Its broken sides were razor-sharp and Cai carefully stowed it inside the food container. Antonia examined Star's nose. She had a deep scratch across the top and blood oozed from the wound, mixing with the sour tomato ketchup. Star shook her head and blood spun into the water.

"Hold still," said Antonia. She put her hands along the cut and imagined it healing. *Mend*.

In her mind, Antonia saw the wound closing up.

Suddenly, a warm feeling spread down her hands and into her fingers. Then, as her fingers started tingling, Antonia pressed more firmly down on the wound.

Heal.

The tingling sensation gave way to a warm glow that spread through Antonia's hands. She held them on Star's nose for a minute longer, then carefully pulled them away. There were ketchup stains on Star's face, but her nose had healed, only a faint line showing where the cut had been.

"Bubbly!" squeaked Bubbles, slapping his tail on the water. "Well done, Silver Dolphin."

"Cai helped too," said Antonia generously. He might not be able to heal animals magically, but she was anxious that Cai's part in the rescue was recognised.

"Thanks, Silver Dolphin," said Bubbles, high-fiving him with a fin.

Spirit, then Dream, rubbed their noses against Cai's and Antonia's, and Star stroked Antonia's hair with a fin. "Thank you, Silver Dolphin."

"It was nothing," said Antonia modestly, although her hands were as limp as an old pair of socks and she was suddenly very tired.

Bubbles started to laugh. Soon he was rolling barrel-like in the water, his mouth open in a wide smile.

"What?" asked Cai.

"Mum," chuckled Bubbles. "She's always warning us to be careful, when really she's the one who should take more care."

Spirit and Dream burst out laughing, and even Star smiled. "So I was right to fuss," she clicked. "Accidents happen when you least expect them."

Bubbles and Dream clicked with laughter until Spirit called them to order. "The Silver Dolphins haven't finished their work. There's the rubbish to clear up from the eelgrass beds."

"Can we help the Silver Dolphins?" asked Bubbles.

"Please, Dad?" added Dream.

Spirit shook his head. "One accident is enough. The Silver Dolphins are more used to glass than we are. Besides, your mother needs to rest. We must return to the pod."

"Sorry, Silver Dolphins!" Bubbles sighed. "Next time, we'll help you."

Antonia and Cai watched as the dolphins swam away. They were a magnificent sight – four silver arrows leaping in and out of the sea in a sparkling fountain of water.

"Back to work," said Antonia when the dolphins had become fast-moving specks in the distance.

They dived down to inspect the eelgrass beds, passing a pile of cans that Spirit and Star had already moved out of harm's way. Cai reached out to pick up a bottle and startled a pair of seahorses hidden in the vegetation. They flitted quickly in the opposite direction. Antonia stared in delight, loving their miniature shape and the way their necks curved like real horses.

"They're beautiful."

She would have loved to touch one, but knew she couldn't. "We must look like giant monsters to them," Antonia added, making Cai chuckle.

They cleared up the litter in silence, until Cai picked up a glass bottle, now full of sea water.

"Definitely a party," he commented.

"But where was it held?" asked Antonia. "The beach is tiny and you can't reach it unless you come by boat."

Cai picked up another bottle. "There's a shell stuck in this one," he said, upending it so the shell plopped out. "I think the rubbish must have been thrown from the top of the cliff."

"Then we must find out who's doing it and make them stop," said Antonia. "The seahorses won't stand a chance if this continues."

"Good idea. Let's go for a walk on the cliffs when we've finished here," said Cai.

Antonia shook her head.

"It's going to take ages to shift this lot and

I promised Mum I'd be home for tea. She might ground me again if I'm late."

"Do you want me to go on my own?"

"No," squeaked Antonia. "I want to come too. We could go tomorrow morning, if you're free?"

"OK," said Cai. "Meet me at Sea Watch first. Come early and I'll ask Aunty Claudia to cook us bacon sandwiches before we start."

Chapter Nine

"There you go," said Claudia, setting down a plate stacked with freshly-cooked bacon sandwiches and handing round mugs of tea.

"Thanks." Antonia moved the map that she and Cai had been studying. "Mmm, these look delicious."

"Just what we need before we go out

catching villains," agreed Cai.

Putting down her own mug of tea, Claudia regarded him sternly.

"You are not to catch anyone. If you find out who is throwing rubbish into the sea, then you come straight back and tell me."

Cai gave her a cheeky grin. "I knew that really."

"Seriously," Claudia continued. "Promise me you won't take matters into your own hands. If you discover anything, then let me deal with it. I'll pass the information on to Jack, the coastguard. That's what he's here for."

"I promise," said Cai.

There was a small silence, then changing the subject, Claudia asked, "Did Jessica enjoy herself when she came and helped out last week?"

"I think so." Antonia shifted uncomfortably, remembering Jessica's unhappy face earlier that morning when she'd learnt Antonia was going to Sea Watch again.

"But I wanted you to go swimming with me," she'd wailed.

"You can come to Sea Watch," Antonia offered generously.

"No!" Furiously, Jessica scratched her head until her hair stood up like a troll's. "I want to practise my swimming."

"Jessica, stop scratching. Get a brush and I'll comb your hair," said Mum. "And then, if you're good, we'll phone Naomi and see if she wants to come round."

Naomi was happy to come over, but Jessica still glared at Antonia when she went out, and Antonia felt guilty and uneasy. Jessica had been keen to improve her swimming for a while, but why the sudden desperation?

Antonia and Cai stacked the dishwasher for Claudia while she filled up two drinking bottles with water and found some crisps and apples to keep them going until lunchtime.

"Don't go dropping rubbish," she said, smiling, as she packed everything into a small rucksack and handed it to Cai.

"As if!" he snorted.

According to the map, the cove with the seahorse colony lay between Claudia's beach and Sandy Bay. The Coastal Path, a public footpath, ran along the cliffs above it. It was another scorching hot day and by the time they got to the top of the cliffs, they were ready for a break. Cai sunk to the ground, rummaged in his rucksack, then pulled out the bottles of water. Antonia swigged hers gratefully, letting the ice-cold water trickle slowly down her throat.

"It's not that far now," said Cai. "I think I recognise where we are, even though it looks different seeing it from up here instead of down there."

"Careful," warned Antonia. "Don't go any closer to the edge, in case it crumbles."

She stood next to him and they both stared out to sea until, hearing footsteps, Antonia spun round. A tall boy in his late teens was stomping along the path. He wore a dark

green hoodie with the hood pulled up over his head.

"He must be roasting in that," whispered Cai.

Shoulders rounded, hands in pockets, the boy slouched towards them. Antonia felt the hairs on her neck bristle. There was something about the boy that she found unsettling. Maybe it was his dirty crumpled clothes. Judging from the state of him, he'd been wearing them for days.

There was a sudden pounding of feet and a second boy rounded a curve in the path at a run.

"Oi, Dwain," he yelled. "Wait up."

Green Hoodie grunted something unintelligible, but waited while his friend, dressed in jeans and a red hoodie, caught up.

"Going fer breakfast? Yer might 'ave waited."

"Waitin' now, ain't I?" muttered Green Hoodie.

Antonia and Cai stifled giggles and when the two boys were out of earshot, Cai grunted, "Oi, Toni. Wanna check out where they came from?"

"If yer want," Antonia agreed, with a chuckle. Unconsciously, her fingers strayed to her dolphin charm. It felt soft and warm and filled her with hope.

"Do you think they're the ones dumping the rubbish?"

"Let's go and find out," said Cai.

A short way along, the path curved again

and the ground to their right rose up in wide steps of land. A two-man tent was pitched on the lower step, its doorway facing out to sea. The flaps were down, so it was impossible to see inside. Warily, Cai and Antonia circled the tent, shocked by the rubbish piled behind it.

"Look at all these bottles," whispered Antonia.

"Yuk, a half-eaten takeaway," said Cai, holding his nose.

"And another supermarket trolley! What's that doing here?"

"I bet they took it to carry those drink bottles," said Cai in disgust.

The tent sounded empty. With a racing heart, Antonia crept round to the front and, lifting a flap, slowly undid the zip. Stale air swirled out, making her cough. Two rumpled sleeping bags lay in a heap and two rucksacks spewed their contents on to the floor.

"Ew! This could be where the rubbish is coming from," she said. "Do you think those boys are on holiday?"

"It looks like it," said Cai. "They're not allowed to camp here, though. Let's go back and tell Aunty Claudia, so she can get them moved on."

The way home was mostly downhill. They ran and slid along the Coastal Path, anxious not to get caught by Green Hoodie and his friend returning from breakfast.

Back at Sea Watch, Claudia phoned Jack the coastguard. She was smiling by the time she ended the call.

"Well done," she congratulated Antonia and Cai. "Jack's going up to see those boys straight away. I also told him about the seahorse colony and he thinks he might be able to get the area classified as a conservation site. It won't happen overnight, but it's a start."

"Wicked!" said Cai, high-fiving Antonia. "That was easily sorted."

"Good," said Antonia, thinking of Jessica and wishing all of her problems were that simple.

Claudia went off to check on the guillemots and decided that they were ready to be released back into the wild. She asked Cai, Antonia and Emily if they would like to help her.

"We'll do it early tomorrow morning," she said. "Before too many people are about."

Emily was thrilled to be invited along and her excitement was catching. Soon Antonia forgot about her anxieties. Her good mood lasted for the whole day and through to breakfast the following morning.

"Jessica, is your head itching?" asked Mum, plonking a weak cup of tea in front of her.

"Yes," said Jessica, scratching furiously.

"Go and get me a comb."

Jessica slid out of her seat and was back in minutes.

"Come over here, away from the table." Deftly, Mum began to part Jessica's hair into sections. "Hmmm, no wonder you're itchy, sweetheart. You have head lice."

"Head lice!" squawked Jessica.

"Calm down. It's nothing to worry about. I can only see a couple, anyway. I'll pop into town as soon as the chemist opens and get you some special shampoo. We'll wash yours in it too, Antonia."

"Me? But I'm fine," Antonia protested. "My hair's not itching."

"Maybe not now, but you may have eggs waiting to hatch," said Mum. "Better to be on the safe side."

"You can't wash it this morning, there isn't time," said Antonia anxiously. "We're releasing the guillemots first thing."

"You're not going anywhere until I've washed your hair," said Mum firmly.

"But Mum—"

"No buts," said Mum. "Claudia won't want you at Sea Watch if there's a chance you've got head lice. You can go later, when you've been treated."

Antonia groaned, knowing there was no point arguing with Mum once she'd made up her mind. It was so unfair. Why did Jessica have to catch head lice now!

Chapter Ten

It wasn't fair to blame Jessica for the head lice, but it took Antonia a lot of effort not to be grumpy with her. Poor Jessica was so miserable and she couldn't stop scratching her head. Antonia finished her breakfast quickly, then telephoned Sea Watch to let them know she wouldn't be coming until later and to wish everyone luck with releasing the birds. She was glad she did. Claudia assured her there would be no great guillemot release until she arrived.

"Just get here when you can," she said.

Antonia cheered up immediately. She was so pleased that she wasn't going to miss the birds being released, that she offered to stay at home with Jessica while Mum walked into town to buy shampoo. In no time, she was back and ready to start the hairwashing. Antonia leant over the bath while her mother held the shower hose, warming the water to a comfortable temperature.

"Better take your necklace off," said Mum.

"But I wear it all the time," Antonia replied, her fingers lightly brushing the dolphin charm.

"The special shampoo might spoil it." Mum turned the shower hose off. "Please, darling."

Antonia didn't want to take her charm off, but Mum refused to wash her hair until she did. Reluctantly, she unfastened the necklace, then looked around the bathroom for somewhere safe to put it.

"Put it in your bedroom," said Mum impatiently.

Jessica was hanging around outside the bathroom. "Are you done already?" she asked, her eyes wide in surprise.

"Do I look done?" asked Antonia shortly, climbing the stairs to her attic room.

She hung her necklace on the blue and gold dolphin that Sophie had bought her, then dashed back to the bathroom.

The shampoo smelt disgusting. Mum washed Antonia's hair a second time in ordinary shampoo and then combed it through with conditioner.

"All done," she said finally. "Not a louse or egg in sight."

"Told you," grumbled Antonia. "Can I go to Sea Watch now?"

"Not until you've dried your hair. Your turn, Jess," Mum called.

Antonia borrowed the hair dryer from her parents' room. She tipped her head upside down and blasted her hair with it on full power.

"I'm off now," she called through the bathroom door, hoping Mum wouldn't come out and notice her hair was still very damp.

"Have a good time," Mum shouted back.

Relieved not to get caught out, Antonia ran downstairs and out of the house as fast as she could. She raced all the way to Sea Watch, arriving out of breath and with a stitch.

Antonia, Cai and Emily put the guillemots into the special cardboard carriers with handles and air holes, while Claudia gave last-minute instructions to Sally, an adult volunteer who was being left in charge. The birds mewed noisily as they were loaded into Claudia's car.

"Hush," soothed Antonia. "Not long now and you'll be free to go wherever you want."

"That's amazing," said Emily as the birds quietened. "It's like they understand you."

Claudia drove the birds to a cliff-top

location, away from the more touristy spots. A light breeze caught Antonia's hair as she climbed out of the car. She pushed it back off her face. Her neck felt strangely bare. Antonia's hand flew to her throat. Her silver dolphin charm wasn't there! In her rush to get out of the house she'd forgotten to put it back on. Antonia almost howled with dismay. How could she have been so stupid? What if Spirit called her?

She glanced across at Cai. His face was flushed with excitement as he helped Claudia lift the bird carriers carefully from the car. Pinned to his T-shirt, his silver dolphin badge winked in the sunshine. Antonia took a deep breath. She had to stay calm. Panicking wouldn't help. If Spirit called now, then she

would know because she would hear Cai's charm. Once the birds had been released, she would nip home and get her necklace. There would only be a short time when she wasn't in contact with a silver dolphin charm.

But Antonia still felt uneasy. The charm was so important that she felt like she was missing a part of herself. She shivered and tried to ignore the bad feeling wedged in her stomach.

"Antonia, are you ready?" Claudia called.

Forcing a smile, Antonia went and stood by Cai and Emily.

"There's one container each," said Claudia. "I'll do the first one. Quiet now, everyone."

She turned the largest bird carrier on its side to allow the birds to hop out, then deftly opened the lid. There were three guillemots inside. At first they stayed where they were, mistrustful. Warily, the smallest hopped forward. Everyone stood very still. The guillemot took another step and peered outside. Then, flapping his black and white feathers, he flew away. He was quickly followed by his two cellmates.

"Hooray!" cheered Cai. "Can I let the next ones go?"

The other containers held two birds each. Cai's birds flew away quickly and so did Emily's. She was so busy watching hers circling in the sky that she accidentally tripped over the empty container. She landed on her bottom, making everyone laugh.

"Clumsy as ever," said Emily, cheerfully

shoving her glasses further up her nose.

Then it was Antonia's turn. She felt uncomfortable as all eyes turned her way. Would Claudia and Cai notice she wasn't wearing her silver dolphin charm? Antonia let her long blonde hair swing over her neck as she carefully put the container on its side and opened it up. Both her birds hopped straight out and, with a thankful mew, they took off. Antonia gathered up the empty containers and took them back to the car.

"Is everything all right?" asked Claudia, following her.

"Yes, fine thanks," Antonia blustered.

Gently, Claudia turned her round so they were facing. Her sea-green eyes searched Antonia's face.

Something's troubling you.

Antonia felt slightly dizzy with the intensity of Claudia's thoughts.

I'm fine, honestly.

She didn't sound convincing, even to herself. Scared that Claudia might probe deeper and discover her guilty secret, Antonia imagined she was standing in front of an enormous brick wall. She felt a warm buzz as Claudia tried to send her another thought, but she concentrated on the wall until the buzzing stopped. Claudia's eyes widened. She opened her mouth as if to say something, then changed her mind. Taking Antonia's hand, she squeezed it lightly.

"You know I'm always here for you, Silver Dolphin." She spoke softly and Antonia had to

strain to hear. Claudia squeezed her hand again. Antonia's stomach churned and she felt slightly sick. Part of her wanted to confess to Claudia that she wasn't wearing her charm, but she couldn't. She was too ashamed. She knew she'd let everyone down.

Back at Sea Watch, the place felt sadly empty without the guillemots. There was lots of work to do, cleaning up both the inside and outside pens they'd lived in. Claudia asked Cai and Antonia to make a start on the indoor pens, as they were the dirtiest.

"I've just got to go home for something," said Antonia. "I won't be long."

"Skiver," said Cai good-naturedly. "Any excuse not to help with the smelly jobs."

Claudia said nothing, but Antonia could

feel her curiosity as strongly as if she had asked a long list of questions.

She left the Sea Watch building quickly. The day was getting hotter. As Antonia ran towards home, she wished she could turn into a Silver Dolphin whenever she wanted to, instead of when she was needed. Then she could have swum most of the way home. She touched her neck, shuddering at its bareness. Right now, she couldn't turn into a Silver Dolphin at all. The thought made her run even faster. She arrived home gasping for breath and with a burning pain in her lungs.

"Antonia," called Mum, as she let herself indoors. "You're back early. Is everything all right?"

"Fine," Antonia panted, using her last dregs

of energy to hop upstairs. "I forgot something."

She pushed open her bedroom door and crossed the room, her hand outstretched to take her necklace from the blue and gold dolphin on her dressing table. Halfway there she stopped. Her eyes widened in disbelief. The statue was empty. Her silver dolphin charm had gone.

Chapter Eleven

A scream rose in her throat. Grimly, she forced it back.

"Mum," she called, moving to the door. "Have you moved my dolphin necklace?"

"I can't hear you. I'm in the kitchen if you want me," Mum called back.

Antonia raced downstairs. Mum was

making sandwiches for lunch. Jessica sat at the table watching her and munching on a carrot stick.

"I can't find my dolphin necklace. It's gone!"

"Gone? Are you sure?" asked Mum, calmly cutting bread into triangles.

"Yes!" Antonia's voice rose. "I hung it on the dolphin Sophie gave me, but it's not there now. Jess, did you take it?"

"No." Jessica's tone was surly. "Why would I?"

"Jess, this is important." Antonia bent down so she was looking straight at her sister. "I won't be cross with you, if you did. I just need it back."

"Antonia!" Mum exclaimed. "Don't question

Jessica like that. She already told you she hasn't taken your necklace."

"Well, where is it then?" asked Antonia. "I *definitely* left it in my room."

"Then it must still be there," said Mum evenly. "You can't have looked properly."

"I have. I know exactly where I left it and it's not there now!" Antonia was so full of fear and frustration, she thought she might explode.

"If I had a pound for every time you girls claimed to have mislaid something, then I wouldn't need to work," said Mum. "Go and have another look."

Jessica finished her carrot stick and picked up another. She began to eat, studying it very carefully as she chewed. Antonia stared at

her. Jessica wasn't usually this quiet. Was this a guilty silence?

"Jess..." Antonia wanted to ask her if she was telling the truth, but a warning look from Mum silenced her. Stiffly, she exited the kitchen and went to her room to search again. It was a waste of time. Even as Antonia emptied drawers and her big cupboard, she knew she wouldn't find the necklace. Her sixth sense told her it wasn't there.

When Antonia finished, it looked like a tornado had passed through her room. She stared out of the window, watching Jessica eating sandwiches in the garden with Mum. Antonia itched to search her sister's room, but knew Mum and Jessica would go mad if they caught her. Her stomach rumbled, reminding her of the packed lunch she'd left at Sea Watch. Antonia realised she must head back there; Cai would be waiting for her. And Cai was her only link to Spirit. Unless… Claudia didn't really need her silver dolphin charm now she had retired. Would she lend it to Antonia? And was she brave enough to ask Claudia for such a big favour? Leaving her room exactly as it was, Antonia ran downstairs to tell Mum she was going back to Sea Watch.

The volunteers were finishing lunch when she arrived.

"Are you all right?" Cai asked quietly. "You were gone ages."

"I'm fine, thanks," said Antonia. She was tempted to confess that she'd lost her necklace. But surely she ought to tell Claudia first?

"Aunty Claudia was worried about you too. But I knew you'd tell us if something was bothering you." Cai's dark eyes challenged Antonia.

"Of course. Where is Claudia? I could do with a chat."

"She had to go out. She got a call from a tourist who'd seen a sick seal over towards Newport. She left Sally in charge."

"Oh!" Could the day get any worse? Antonia didn't cry easily, but tears were gathering in her eyes and threatening to run down her face. Swallowing, she brushed them away.

"Do you want to go somewhere more private?" asked Cai.

"Yes," said Antonia, deciding she must tell him her shocking news. "Let's go and sit on the beach."

Cai was really kind about the lost necklace and immediately offered to lend Antonia his charm.

"You can't do that!" Antonia exclaimed, but her heartbeat quickened.

"It makes sense," insisted Cai. "You're a much more powerful Silver Dolphin than I am. If there's an emergency, you'll be better at dealing with it."

Antonia hesitated. Cai was right, but was it fair to stop him from answering the dolphin's call because of her own carelessness? If only she'd not been in such a hurry, she'd have remembered to put her necklace back on.

Then there wouldn't have been a problem.

Sensing her dilemma, Cai said, "I bet Aunty Claudia would think it was a good idea. And I could borrow hers. She lent it to me once before."

"Yes, but that was different," said Antonia. "She lent it to you because she wanted to know if you were a Silver Dolphin."

She sat with her back against the Sea Watch boat, scrunching up the gritty sand with her bare feet as she thought about Claudia. What would she say? The answer came to her in a flash – Claudia's voice in her head.

Go and work it out.

It was what Claudia always said in a crisis. Antonia concentrated on Claudia, picturing her kindly face with its sea-green eyes, framed by her unruly curls.

I'm sorry. I let you down.

You haven't.

But I've lost my charm.

Believe in yourself, Silver Dolphin.

Antonia thought she heard a chuckle, then her head was silent. Claudia often told Antonia to believe in herself and it helped her to make up her mind.

"Thanks, Cai, but I'm not going to take your charm," she said. "I'm going to find mine."

Her words came back to haunt her later that night as she lay wide awake in bed, staring at the stars through her sloping bedroom window. Earlier in the evening, she'd carefully put her things away until her bedroom was tidy again, but she didn't find the silver dolphin necklace. Try as she did to stop herself, Antonia strongly suspected that Jessica had taken it. Her little sister had swung between being secretive and bubbling with excitement, all evening. She was going to the beach with Naomi and her mum the following day and had begged Antonia to go with them.

"I've not been invited, Jess," Antonia protested.

"You don't need an invitation to go to the beach," said Jessica. "Please come and watch me swim."

Eventually, to get some peace, Antonia promised to go down to the beach before she went to Sea Watch. Afterwards, she'd

126

regretted her decision. What had she been thinking? She had to get to Sea Watch early to be near Cai. It had been bad enough spending a whole evening away from him, even though Cai had assured her he would ring if he got a call from Spirit. Maybe she should break her promise and not go and watch Jessica. Antonia climbed out of bed and stood in front of her open window. In the dark, the sea looked like an enormous black lake. Where were her dolphins now? Knowing she was powerless to hear them if they called for help, Antonia hoped they were safe, somewhere out at sea.

Chapter Twelve

The next morning, Antonia woke with a hollow feeling inside her. Her fingers crept to her neck, seeking reassurance in her dolphin charm. They found nothing. Immediately, Antonia struggled up, pushing her duvet away as yesterday's awfulness came rushing back. Her silver dolphin necklace was missing and she had no way of hearing Spirit's call. Before she dressed, Antonia checked her room once more in the hope that her necklace might have reappeared as mysteriously as it had vanished. But it hadn't. Disappointed, she went downstairs for breakfast.

Jessica was already halfway through a bowl of cereal.

"Hello," she mumbled.

Antonia studied her sister. She seemed nervous and kept yawning as if she hadn't slept properly.

"Hi, Jess. Where are Mum and Dad?"

"Dad's in the bathroom; Mum's taken him up a mug of tea. Don't forget you said you'd come to the beach and watch me swim today."

"Er… I'm going to Sea Watch. But I could

come to the beach later. How long are you going for?"

"All day," said Jessica. She pushed her cereal bowl away from her. "You promised you'd come."

She looked so fierce, Antonia decided she couldn't break her promise after all.

"I'll be there," she agreed.

"Good," said Jessica. "Cos I'm going to surprise you."

She shot Antonia a triumphant look, then pushing back her chair, went upstairs to her room.

Antonia sat down. What did Jessica mean by surprising her? Antonia was so deep in thought, she didn't hear her mother come into the kitchen and switch on the kettle.

"Antonia, I asked if you wanted a cup of tea."

"Oh! Sorry, I didn't hear you. Yes, please," said Antonia.

She drank the tea and nibbled on a piece of toast. She didn't really want either, but no way would Mum let her go out unless she'd eaten something. Antonia wondered if she should challenge her sister again over the missing necklace. It was worth a try. Sighing heavily, she dumped her mug and plate in the dishwasher, then went to her sister's room. The door wouldn't open. None of the bedroom doors had locks, so Jessica must have wedged something against it. She'd never done that before!

"Jess, it's me. Can I come in?"

"No, I'm not ready. Go away." Jessica sounded alarmed.

"Ready for what?"

"Going out with Naomi. I haven't got my swimming stuff together. You won't forget to come to the beach, will you?"

"I won't forget. Jess, I…" Antonia hesitated before adding, "I'm going to look for my necklace. If you see it, you will tell me, won't you?"

There was a moment of silence before Jessica answered crossly, "Yes."

Antonia stood for a bit, listening to her sister furtively creeping around her room. Jessica wasn't giving anything away. Despondently, Antonia collected her packed lunch from the kitchen and went to Sea Watch.

Claudia wasn't there again. Sensing Antonia's disappointment, Cai said awkwardly, "I told Aunty Claudia about your dolphin charm and asked if I should lend you mine, but she said no. She wasn't cross with you or anything. She was smiling."

"It's OK," said Antonia. Claudia was probably amused because she'd known about the charm before he told her. Cai wasn't aware of the telepathy between Antonia and Claudia. Antonia hadn't told him because she didn't want Cai to think she was boasting. Idly, she wondered why Claudia hadn't wanted Cai to lend her his own charm, or offered to lend Antonia hers. Was it because she didn't trust her not to lose it?

Believe in yourself.

Remembering Claudia's words, Antonia grinned. Of course Claudia still trusted her.

Even with the guillemots gone, there was plenty to do at Sea Watch. Claudia was organising a litter-picking day on the beach for the public and needed posters to advertise the event. The poster makers – Antonia, Emily, Karen, Eleanor and new volunteers, Eddie and Oliver – sat round the big table sharing coloured pens and chatting.

Antonia tried to relax and enjoy the company, but she was more wound up than an old-fashioned clock. She only had one ear for conversation. The other was busy listening out for Cai's silver dolphin charm. At mid morning, when Sally called to the volunteers for a tea break, Antonia excused herself. It was time to go to Sandy Bay and watch Jessica swim. She half hoped that Cai might offer to go with her. But he didn't, and Antonia didn't invite him along because then he would have felt obliged to go with her even if he didn't want to.

Sandy Bay beach was heaving with holiday-makers. Antonia sat on the promenade, scanning the crowd for Jessica, while she took off her sandals. The lifeguards had erected two flags on the beach, marking out a safe area for bathers to swim. Guessing that her little sister would be somewhere between the two flags, Antonia headed in that direction. Jessica must have been watching out for her. She suddenly leapt up, shouting and waving her beach towel. Antonia waved back. Jessica dropped the towel and began an earnest conversation with Mrs Simmons, Naomi's mum. Then she and Naomi headed towards the sea. Mrs Simmons stood up and waved at Antonia before hurrying after the two girls. Antonia hopped across the beach and left her shoes by Jessica's screwed-up towel. As she continued down to the sea, a familiar sensation washed over her, making her body tingle with anticipation. Antonia stopped dead and her hands flew to her bare neck. Spirit was about to call. But how would she know for definite when that call came? Another startling thought occurred to her. Why had Jessica suddenly rushed into the sea? Antonia stared after her little sister, now jumping through the surf. Why was she in such a hurry?

Chapter Thirteen

ntonia remained where she was, unsure what to do. If Spirit was about to call, should she run back to Sea Watch to meet Cai? But what if she didn't make it in time and he answered the call *without* her? Could she become a Silver Dolphin without being near his charm? Antonia's eyes focused on the sea again. Jessica was easily identifiable in her bright pink costume, swimming with jerky movements towards the orange safety buoy. Naomi had stopped when the sea reached her waist. She must have swallowed some water because her mum was patting her on the back. Suddenly, Mrs Simmons noticed that Jessica had gone on without them and she shouted for her to wait. Jessica kept swimming until she was level with the orange safety buoy. Then, waving a hand, she swam past it.

"Jessica!" gasped Antonia. It was an unbreakable rule in the Lee household that no one went further than the orange safety buoy. Was Jessica showing off? Antonia was too concerned for her sister's safety to be impressed by how far she'd swum.

Suddenly, a high-pitched whistle sounded in Antonia's head. It was so unexpected, it made her wince. The whistle was followed by a series of clicks.

Silver Dolphin. Come quickly!

Shocked to hear Spirit's voice so clearly in her head, Antonia almost didn't answer him.

Spirit?

Hurry, Silver Dolphin!

But how? I've lost my magic charm.

Believe in yourself. Believe you can.

All at once, a fog cleared in Antonia's head. She remembered talking to Claudia when she first became a Silver Dolphin. Claudia had told her that the necklace was a receiver. It was a way for Spirit to communicate with the

Silver Dolphins. But she'd also said that to turn into a Silver Dolphin, you only had to believe in the magic. So Antonia didn't need her charm to become a Silver Dolphin! And now, to her amazement, Antonia was communicating with Spirit without even wearing her charm. No wonder Claudia wasn't worried when Antonia told her that she'd lost it. She must have known all along that Antonia was such a powerful Silver Dolphin, she didn't need it!

A sudden scream brought her sharply back to the beach. It was Jessica – she was in trouble! She was thrashing about and her head kept disappearing under the water.

Hurry, Silver Dolphin!

Antonia froze. Here was double danger.

Both Spirit and Jessica needed her help. Antonia's brain raced. Mrs Simmons was already in the water, but she was helping Naomi. There were two lifeguards on duty. But this was her sister.

Still dressed in her shorts and T-shirt, Antonia ran into the sea. The moment she swam, her clothes filled with water, pulling her back. Frustrated by her wet clothes, Antonia struggled on. She felt bad about ignoring Spirit, but was terrified for Jess. Would she reach her sister in time? A whisper stole into her confused thoughts. It was a sound she'd heard several times before, when Spirit called, only this time it was clearer. Antonia listened to it as she swam. The whispering was growing louder. Gradually, it

turned into a familiar voice.

Spirit. I hear your call.

Antonia was so astonished, she almost stopped swimming. She heard Spirit's voice next, urging Cai to come quickly, then his reply.

I'm on my way.

Cai?

No reply. No matter how hard Antonia tried, she couldn't make Cai hear her. Never mind. It was brilliant that she'd heard him. She swam on, feeling better now she knew that Cai was answering Spirit's call.

The gap between her and Jessica was closing. Scared she wouldn't get to her quickly enough, Antonia forced herself to swim even faster. She reached Jessica just as her sister disappeared under the water and didn't resurface. Diving down, Antonia grabbed the back of her bright pink costume. She hauled Jessica upwards until they both surfaced. Jessica spluttered and coughed up water. Quickly, Antonia hooked her left arm round her sister's chest.

"You're safe now," she said.

Jessica struggled, but Antonia held her firmly. "Jess, it's me, Antonia. Relax. I've got you."

"Antonia!" sobbed Jessica. Swallowing another mouthful of salty water, she began coughing and retching.

"Sssh," said Antonia soothingly. "Relax. I'm going to tow you ashore."

Antonia kicked her legs and paddled with

her free hand. The life-saving lessons she'd had at her swimming club quickly came back to her. It was awkward towing someone almost as big as you, but Antonia was a strong swimmer and little by little, she towed her sister nearer to the beach. Jessica was sobbing uncontrollably.

"It didn't work," she hiccupped. "It stopped working. My legs hurt and I couldn't breathe."

"Hush," said Antonia, with no spare breath to talk.

As she approached other swimmers, people came to help her: Mrs Simmons, a boy in an inflatable dinghy and one of the lifeguards carrying a swimming float. The lifeguard offered Antonia the float, but she shook her head. She allowed him to take Jessica from her, though. She swam alongside him, murmuring words of comfort to her sister. When the water was shallow enough to walk, the lifeguard scooped Jessica up into his arms and carried her ashore. He took her straight to the first-aid trailer that was parked at the top of the beach. Antonia, Mrs Simmons and Naomi followed, Antonia's wet clothes squelching uncomfortably.

There was a small stretcher bed inside the trailer and the lifeguard laid Jessica on it, covering her with a thick grey blanket. "We'll call an ambulance," he said, reaching for a mobile phone. "What's your name, sweetheart? Jessica. That's a pretty name."

"Don't want to go to hospital," muttered Jessica.

"Well, you seem fine, but you've had quite a shock. It's best to let the hospital check you over."

The lifeguard rang for an ambulance and then for Mrs Lee, who said she would come straight away. Then, after rummaging in a small cupboard, he handed out towels.

"Well done you," he said to Antonia, handing her the biggest one. "Hero of the day. You saved Jessica's life."

"She's my sister," said Antonia, wiping a strand of wet hair away from Jessica's face.

Jessica was crying again. She mumbled something and Antonia bent her head to hear her.

"I'm sorry," she sobbed. "I didn't steal it. I only wanted to borrow it. But it didn't work properly. The good luck magic ran out."

Suddenly, noticing the silver dolphin necklace hanging round Jessica's neck, Antonia's eyes widened. So she'd been right all along! Jessica had taken it.

"Oh, Jess!" said Antonia. "I told you before. There's only one way to improve your swimming. That's by practising."

"I'm sorry." Jessica struggled up and, propping herself on an elbow, unfastened Antonia's chain.

As the dolphin charm dropped into Antonia's hand, she felt it vibrating. Her eyes flew to Jessica. She was still looking at the necklace, but she didn't seem to notice that

it was moving. So Jessica wasn't a Silver Dolphin after all. Antonia felt a mixture of relief and guilt. A sharp whistle echoed round the trailer. Then Spirit's voice clicked inside her head.

Silver Dolphin. Come quickly!

No one was taking any notice of the ear-splitting noise. Mrs Simmons was talking with the lifeguard and Naomi was munching on a bar of chocolate he'd given her.

"Do you forgive me?" asked Jessica.

Antonia was so happy to have her necklace back, she would have forgiven her sister most things, right then. She fastened it round her own neck. The dolphin's tail began to beat. Faster and faster it went. Startled by its intensity, Antonia covered it with her hand.

Was this the same call for help or a new one?
Jessica's lip began to tremble.

"Please will you forgive me?"

"Of course I will," said Antonia. "Listen, Jess, I've got something important to do. Will you be all right if I leave you with Naomi and Mrs Simmons? Mum'll be here soon."

Jessica nodded bravely.

"Thanks." Antonia bent down and hugged her. "I wish I was going to the hospital with you. What fun to ride in an ambulance! When you get home, you can tell me all about it."

Chapter Fourteen

ntonia headed for the rocks at the furthest end of Sandy Bay beach. There were a few people there with nets, but they were too busy catching shrimps in the rock pools to notice her as she waded into the sea, fully dressed. As soon as the water was deep enough, Antonia swam, with flipper hands.

Immediately, her legs melded together and kicked like a tail. It felt fantastic. Antonia wanted to leap out of the sea, but instead she dived down and swam underwater so as not to draw attention to herself. Spirit's call was coming from the same direction as the seahorse colony.

"Please let the seahorses be safe," she murmured anxiously.

Hurry, Silver Dolphin!

In an emergency, Silver Dolphin magic allowed Antonia to swim exceptionally fast. It was obvious from Spirit's cry that it was urgent.

Spirit, I'm coming, she whistled back.

Antonia sped on, travelling even faster than a real dolphin. The closer to the seahorse

colony she swam, the more her anxiety increased. The elegant seahorses were so fragile. It would be terrible if something else had happened to them. Sensing vibrations above her, Antonia surfaced. She'd swum further than she realised and the seahorse colony was only a short distance ahead. Spirit, Star, Dream and Bubbles were all waiting for her near a cluster of rocks. Movement on the rocks made Antonia glance towards them. Cai was perched on top, struggling with something.

"Silver Dolphin," clicked Spirit. "You came at last."

He briefly rubbed her nose, then nodded his head towards Cai. "It's the eelgrass beds again. Someone's thrown so much rubbish into them, the other Silver Dolphin can't move it all on his own."

Quickly, Antonia swam over to Cai. The rocks were slippery with seaweed and she scraped her knees pulling herself out of the water.

"Thank goodness you're here," said Cai, clearly relieved. He was crouched over a pile of rubbish, stacking it so that it didn't fall back into the sea.

"Those hoodies had one last clear-out before the coastguard moved them on," he said angrily. "It's going to take ages to shift this lot. They've thrown that other supermarket trolley in too – the one we found behind the tent."

"Is there much damage to the eelgrass?" asked Antonia.

"Loads – the trolley caused the most," said Cai. "I found another dead seahorse under one of its wheels."

Antonia gasped. Poor seahorse! "Let's move the trolley next," she said.

Carefully, she jumped off the rocks and into the sea. Cai followed and together they swam to the eelgrass beds. There was litter everywhere. The sight of it made Antonia's heart race with anger.

"What a mess!" she exclaimed.

"And I've already shifted some of it," said Cai grimly.

The trolley was heavy and awkward to move. Antonia's long fingers carefully worked at freeing the eelgrass caught in its wheels.

"I hate repeating a job," she grumbled. "I

wish those hoodies knew what damage they've caused. Maybe they'd think twice before using the sea as a rubbish bin again."

At last the trolley was free and Antonia and Cai swam with it to the surface.

"There's no room for it on the rocks," panted Cai.

"We couldn't lift it up there anyway," said Antonia. "Let's take it back to Sea Watch and get some dustbin bags to put the rest of the rubbish in. It'll be easier to move."

"Good idea," Cai agreed.

They told Spirit their plans. Bubbles and Dream wanted to go with them, but Star wouldn't allow it.

"It's too dangerous. The Silver Dolphins will come back. Swim with them when they

take the next load," she clicked.

Remembering what fun they'd had when they'd swum the bin ashore, Antonia was disappointed. But Star was right. The trolley could be dangerous to a dolphin, and the Silver Dolphins would swim much faster without Bubbles playing about.

Reaching the Sea Watch beach, they dragged the trolley ashore. Water cascaded from their clothes.

"Leave it here," puffed Cai when they were through the beach gate and in Claudia's garden. "We'll move it later. I'll just go and get some bin bags."

Antonia waited impatiently while Cai sprinted up to the house. When he came back, a worried frown creased his face.

"Can we become Silver Dolphins again?" he whispered, even though there was no one around to overhear. "Or does Spirit have to call us?"

"We haven't finished our task yet, so the magic is still working," Antonia quietly answered. "Just remember, believe you're a Silver Dolphin when you enter the water."

"Wicked!" exclaimed Cai.

They ran back down the beach with the bin bags. Cai had a dreamy look on his face as he splashed into the sea. When the water reached his chest, he began to swim. Immediately, his legs melded together like a tail.

"It worked!" he clicked, giving Antonia a delighted grin.

They raced back to the eelgrass beds,

leaping in and out of the water like real dolphins, their bodies curving in graceful arcs.

It took ages to collect all the rubbish and they filled all three bin bags. Once the litter had been cleared, the eelgrass beds looked much better. The trampled stems began to revive and cautiously, the seahorses came out of hiding.

"Look," said Cai, grabbing Antonia's arm.

One of the seahorses was behaving strangely. It thrust its stomach backwards and forwards until suddenly, a tiny ball-like shape popped out of its pouch. It was followed by lots more, and as each ball hit the water, it opened up and wriggled away. Antonia stared in amazement.

"He's giving birth!" she clicked. "Look at all the baby seahorses. They're so small."

The seahorse's stomach kept contracting as more babies squirted from his pouch and into the water. Soon, he'd almost disappeared in a cloud of miniature seahorses. Then the babies quickly swam away. Fascinated, Antonia and Cai watched until the seahorse finished. Then he hovered in the water, as if he was catching his breath.

With shining eyes, Antonia turned to Cai. "Now that was magic!" she exclaimed.

Antonia and Cai swam to the surface with the three bags of rubbish. Bubbles bobbed excitedly in the water.

"Now can we help the Silver Dolphins?" he asked.

"Yes," Spirit agreed. "They look like they need it."

"Don't go too close to the shore," warned Star. "It's busy this time of year. You don't want to draw attention to yourselves."

"Muuuum!" Bubbles and Dream clicked, laughing. "Stop fussing."

Star smiled. "I can't help it," she said good-naturedly. "I only want you to be safe."

"Of course they'll be safe," clicked Spirit. "They're with the Silver Dolphins."

Antonia flushed. Spirit had so much faith in her, even though she'd lost her charm. Would he still trust her if she hadn't managed to answer his call?

There will always be difficult choices, Silver Dolphin.

Spirit made no sound, but Antonia clearly heard his voice inside her head.

I never want to fail you, Antonia replied, not daring to think about what that might mean.

Spirit nudged her with his nose, then gently ruffled her hair with his flipper.

Just always do your best.

Antonia caught her breath.

I will, she promised.

The bags of rubbish were heavy and it was hard work swimming with them to the shore. Antonia wondered if they should have made two journeys, but Bubbles and Dream helped, swimming either side to support the bags. Antonia kept a careful eye on them. In her experience, bin bags often split and she didn't want Bubbles or Dream to be injured by the rubbish. She swam in silence, listening to Bubbles chattering on about all the things

they'd do the next time they were allowed to play. The double drama had been exhausting and the swim home was sapping the last of her energy.

Cai's voice suddenly broke through her thoughts. "You found your charm then?"

"Yes," said Antonia, not mentioning that she didn't need it any more. Maybe she would tell Cai one day, but not yet.

"Where was it?"

"Jessica borrowed it. She thought it would make her swim better."

Cai gasped, then after a bit, he chuckled.

"I've always wanted a brother or sister, but I'd hate it if they took my stuff without asking. I mean, you don't have to share *everything*, do you?"

Possessively, he touched the silver dolphin charm pinned to his T-shirt. Antonia remembered how she'd not wanted to share the secret of the Silver Dolphins with Jessica. Then, suddenly, she had a brainwave. Once the rubbish was safely back at Sea Watch, she had another job to do.

Chapter Fifteen

By the time Claudia's beach came into sight, everyone was flagging.

"Next time we'll play," squeaked Bubbles.

"Definitely," Antonia agreed. "We'll play seaweed tag and Sprat, and you can show me how to do the twister again."

"Bubbly!" said Bubbles, brightening. "I hope

Dad calls you soon."

Bubbles and Dream rubbed noses goodbye with Cai and Antonia. Then they raced away, their bodies arching like silver rainbows as they swam out to sea.

"Not far now," said Antonia, rallying herself.

They swam until they were bumping their knees on the seabed, then, rising out of the surf, they carried the rubbish ashore. Water poured from their clothes as Antonia and Cai struggled up the beach. After a bit, Cai signalled to stop.

"Phew!" he panted, carefully setting the bags down on the sand. "How on earth did we manage to swim this lot ashore?"

He was perfectly dry now, apart from

having slightly damp hair and a wet patch on his T-shirt from carrying the rubbish.

"It's more difficult on land," said Antonia. "Silver Dolphin magic helps us in the water."

They sat for a moment while they got their breath back. The beach gate clicked open. Antonia turned and saw Claudia striding towards them.

"Hello," she said. "What have you got there?"

"Rubbish," said Cai. "A leaving present from the hoodies who were camping on the cliffs."

"What delightful young men," said Claudia grimly. "When Jack went to check that they'd gone, he was very impressed by how tidy they'd left it. If only he knew the truth! Come on then, let's put it in the Sea Watch bins."

They took a bag each.

"We'll come back for our shoes," said Cai, as they reached the Sea Watch boat.

Antonia began to giggle.

"What?" asked Cai.

"My shoes," she chuckled. "I've done it again. I've left them at Sandy Bay beach."

Cai almost choked with laughter. "Oh!" he gasped. "Stop it. I can't breathe. We've got spare towels and gloves in the Sea Watch cupboard. Perhaps we should keep spare shoes too."

"You're getting good at losing things," said Claudia meaningfully, but there was a twinkle in her eye. "Cai's right. I think we'd

better buy a cheap pair of sandals to keep here for emergencies."

"I'll get some today," said Antonia. "I've got to go into town."

Antonia had meant to spend the whole day at Sea Watch, but now there was a more important job she needed to do.

"I'll drive you to Sandy Bay," said Claudia.

"Thanks, but I don't think my shoes will still be there."

And Antonia briefly explained, without sounding too dramatic, how she'd rescued her sister.

"I left my shoes with Jessica's things, so I expect Mum or Mrs Simmons has taken them home for me."

"How are you going to explain leaving your

shoes behind?" asked Cai.

"I don't expect Mum will ask," said Antonia. "She was probably too worried about Jessica to give it much thought."

"You can borrow a pair of my old trainers," said Cai. "Your Mum *will* notice if you go home with bare feet."

"Thanks," said Antonia.

Claudia insisted on running her home in the car and Cai came too.

"Are you coming back?" he asked, as they turned into her road. Antonia nodded. "Definitely. But there's something I need to do first."

Antonia almost regretted her decision to go home. Dad had just driven Mum and Jessica back from the hospital, and they all made a huge fuss of her.

"All those swimming lessons have certainly paid off," said Dad proudly. "You're a hero."

Eventually, Antonia managed to escape up to her room, where she emptied her moneybox. There was quite a bit in it. Antonia was good at saving. She put half the notes and some of the coins into her purse, then put it in the bottom of her shopping bag. Dad had to go back to work, so he offered to drive Antonia into town.

"Thanks," she said gratefully. She was still tired from saving her sister *and* the seahorses.

The shops were full of tourists. Squeezing her way through the crowds, Antonia started at a bargain shop, where she bought a cheap pair of beach shoes. They were perfect for leaving at Sea Watch. Stowing them in her bag, she set off again. She knew what she was looking for, but it took her ages to find exactly the right thing.

Antonia searched shop after shop, her frustration growing. Everything was either far too expensive or wasn't right. She was beginning to despair that she would ever find what she was looking for, when she caught sight of a small jewellery shop down a side street. She slipped down the alley and stood outside with her nose pressed against the window. Her eyes lit up as she spotted it, there in the corner. It was exactly right and at a price she could afford. She hurried inside the shop.

"I'd like to buy the dolphin necklace in the

window, please," she told the shop assistant.

"Certainly," the lady smiled at her. "Is that the silver one?"

"No," said Antonia. "I'd like the gold one, please."

The lady took the chain out of the window and showed it to Antonia. It was perfect. The tiny gold dolphin with its sparkling jewelled eye, looked as if it might suddenly leap off the chain.

"Thanks." Antonia counted out her money.

"Is it for you?" asked the lady, putting the necklace in a small box.

Antonia shook her head. "It's for my sister. To bring her luck," she added.

"It sounds like she's already lucky with a sister like you." The lady beamed at Antonia.

Blushing, Antonia stowed the necklace in her bag and hurried back on to the street. She couldn't wait to see Jessica's face when she gave it to her.

After that, Antonia went into the sweet shop and bought a small bag of chocolate fudge, her favourite flavour. Then, popping a piece in her mouth, she hurried home.

Jessica was in the garden, resting on a sun lounger. She looked really pleased to see Antonia and put aside the book she'd been reading.

"Have you come to play with me?"

"Not today," said Antonia. "You're supposed to be resting. I'll play with you tomorrow."

"Promise?" asked Jessica.

"I promise," said Antonia solemnly. She dug

around in her bag and pulled out the jewellery box. "Here, I got you something in town."

Eagerly, Jessica took it from her.

"What is it?" she asked.

She flipped up the lid and her green eyes widened in surprised delight.

"Oh, Antonia," she whispered. "Thank you."

Looping the chain over her finger, Jessica stared in rapture at the golden dolphin, then gave Antonia a huge hug.

"My very own lucky charm."

"Jessica!" said Antonia in exasperation.

"I know," said Jessica quickly. "I have to practise my swimming. But luck's important too."

Antonia touched her own dolphin charm.

Being a Silver Dolphin was hard work. And although Antonia was getting much better with practice, Jessica was right. Luck was important. Suddenly, her dolphin charm quivered and Antonia's eyes were drawn to the bay. Four dolphins, two large and two small, were leaping through the sea, their bodies making perfect silver arcs.

"Look!" she exclaimed.

Jessica looked up.

"I told you," she said smugly. "My charm is lucky. It's called real dolphins, just for me."

Antonia's charm quivered once more, then was still. She burst out laughing. "Jessica," she giggled. "You do say some funny things."

Silver Dolphins
by Summer Waters

Buy more great Silver Dolphins books from HarperCollins at 10% off recommended retail price. FREE postage and packing in the UK.

Out Now:

Silver Dolphins – The Magic Charm	ISBN: 978-0-00-730968-9
Silver Dolphins – Secret Friends	ISBN: 978-0-00-730969-6
Silver Dolphins – Stolen Treasures	ISBN: 978-0-00-730970-2
Silver Dolphins – Double Danger	ISBN: 978-0-00-730971-9

Coming soon:

Silver Dolphins – Broken Promises	ISBN: 978-0-00-730972-6
Silver Dolphins – Moonlight Magic	ISBN: 978-0-00-730973-3

All priced at £4.99

To purchase by Visa/Mastercard/Switch simply call
08707871724 or fax on **08707871725**